LillyBelle

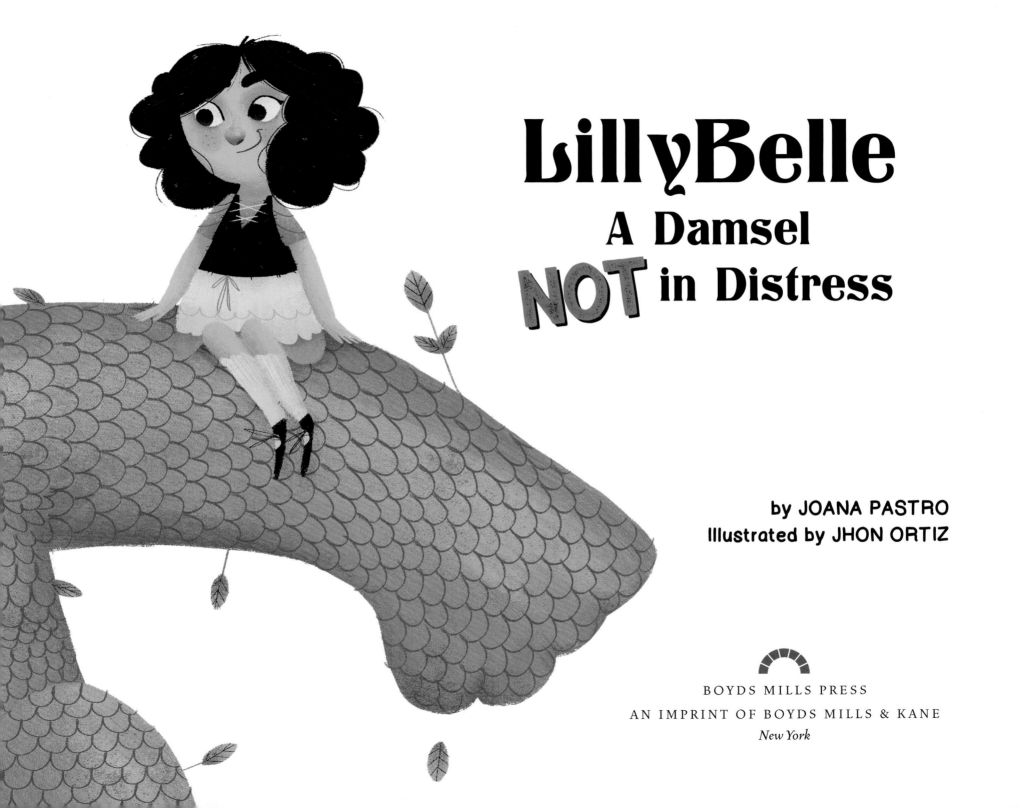

LillyBelle
A Damsel NOT in Distress

by JOANA PASTRO

Illustrated by JHON ORTIZ

BOYDS MILLS PRESS

AN IMPRINT OF BOYDS MILLS & KANE

New York

At Lady Frilly's School for Damsels,
LillyBelle enjoyed:

Baking GLORIOUS cakes.
The taller the better!

Playing MELODIOUS songs.
The louder the better!

Learning SPLENDID manners.
The fancier the better!

And above all, attending tea parties.
Daily, delicious, delightful tea parties.

LillyBelle loved being a damsel but . . .

. . . not being in distress.

Lady Frilly insisted, "A damsel in distress must be captured by a villain, never attempt to escape, and wait patiently for rescue."

LillyBelle didn't like those rules at all. After giving it some thought, she declared, "I'll be a damsel NOT in distress!"

The next morning, LillyBelle was playing hopscotch when, with a terrible cackle, all went . . .

. . . dark.

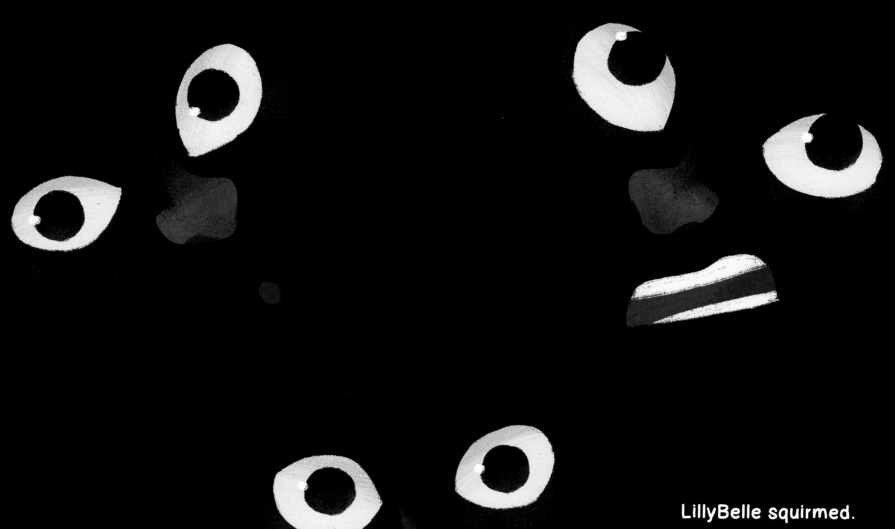

LillyBelle squirmed.
LillyBelle screeched!

She puffed.
She protested!

Until . . .

KERPLUNK!

The witch sugared and sprinkled, tossed and stirred.

A damsel in distress would wait for rescue . . .

. . . I'm a wonderful baker."

So, LillyBelle taught the witch how to bake the most glorious cake. The taller the better!

"It's a monstrosity! I love it!" said the witch.

"And as easy as baking pie!" LillyBelle said.

"Pie?"

"Yes! Perhaps you should try!

Now, if you'll excuse me. The daily, delicious, delightful tea party will start soon.

Too-da-loo!"

LillyBelle was skipping and singing, when gigantic fingers wrapped around her body.

LillyBelle squirmed. LillyBelle screeched!

She puffed. She protested!

Until . . .

KERPLUNK!

"Sing!" the giant demanded.

A damsel in distress would wait for rescue . . .

. . . but not LillyBelle.

"Excuse me, Master Giant.
I see you enjoy listening
to music, but do you know
what's even better?
Singing your own songs!
I happen to be . . .

. . . an excellent voice coach."

LillyBelle taught him a most melodious song.
The louder the better!

And after a dazzling duet, she said,
"Please excuse me. The daily, delicious,
delightful tea party will start soon.

Too-da-loo!"

LillyBelle was prancing along,
picking posies for a beautiful bouquet,
when a big, burly, beastly ogre
threw her over his shoulder.

LillyBelle squirmed.
LillyBelle screeched!

She puffed.
She protested!

Until . . .

KERPLUNK!

The ogre measured and creased,
tied and curled.

A damsel in distress would
wait for rescue . . .

. . . but not LillyBelle.

"Excuse me, Mister Ogre.
Damsels don't make good gifts!
If you wish to impress,
I hear good manners are
all the rage with ogre ladies.
I can teach you,
I'm very . . .

. . . well mannered."

LillyBelle taught him how to say
please and thank you, how to bow,
and other splendid manners.
The fancier the better!

"Please excuse me. I can't be
late for the daily, delicious,
delightful tea party.

Too-da-loo!"

LillyBelle dashed back to school.

Lady Frilly met her outside.
"I've been worried about you!
Were you captured? Who saved you?
A knight? A prince? A ninja?"

"No one. I rescued myself!"
LillyBelle puffed her chest.

"That's impossible! A damsel
in distress cannot escape!"
Lady Frilly said.

Just then, they
heard a cackle,
a high note, and a
"How do you do?"
followed by . . .

"HELP! WE'RE BEING ATTACKED!"

The damsels shrieked and cried.
Some fainted, and others ran for cover . . .

. . . but not LillyBelle.

"Excuse me, ladies. No need to fret.
I happen to be a damsel NOT in distress!"

"Hello, Miss Witch,
Master Giant,
Mister Ogre!

How may I help you?"
she said.

"We're here for the daily, delicious, delightful tea party. I baked a perfect pie!" said the witch.

"I'm here for another dazzling duet," said the giant.

"And I'll display my magnificent manners, thank you very much," said the ogre.

A damsel in distress would lose her wits . . .

. . . **but not LillyBelle.**

"Would you join our tea party?" she asked.

"Yes," said the witch. "Absolutely," said the giant. "Don't mind if I do!" said the ogre.

And everyone had a terrific time . . .

. . . especially
LillyBelle.

To Rodrigo, Leo, Enzo, and Liv,
who have perfect manners . . . most of the time! —J.P.

To my dear mother, Nelly, and my beloved wife, Sofía,
and for all those who encouraged me to fly toward my dreams —J.O.

For information about permission to reproduce selections from this book,
please contact permissions@bmkbooks.com.

Boyds Mills Press
An imprint of Boyds Mills & Kane,
a division of Astra Publishing House
boydsmillspress.com
Printed in the United States of America

ISBN: 978-1-63592-296-7
Library of Congress Control Number: 2019954206

First edition
10 9 8 7 6 5 4 3 2 1

Design by Caitlin Greer
The text is set in 123Marker, BluBerry, Amira, and Luna.
The title is set in Titania and BluBerry Grunge.
The illustrations are done digitally.